My Nanny is a Witch

Written by **Lynsey Tidbury**   Illustrated by **Michelle Catanach**

First published in 2021

For my grandson, James

Let me tell you of my nanny,
My nanny is a Witch.
She is loving kind and gentle.
And has many special gifts.

My nanny is a Witch.
But does not have a pointy hat,
She does not fly a broomstick.
And does not have a black cat.

My nanny is a Witch because she knows about the plants,
She listens to the birdsong,
And she likes to watch the ants.

My nanny likes to teach me about the different kinds of trees,
And how the flower leaves can heal me,
When I fall and scuff my knees.

Nanny also likes to teach me
What to do when I feel bad.
How to breathe into my belly
When I am angry, or I am sad.

Me and Nanny like to sing and dance
And bang a big old drum,
She teaches me old silly songs, we laugh.
It is so much fun.

I often wonder why people say,
That witches are all bad,
All the pictures in the story books,
Just seem wrong and make me sad.

Many, many years ago, the people misunderstood.
They made up stories about witches and said that they
were not good.
They would spread around bad stories about the women
who were wise,
Causing fear amongst the villagers.
But their stories were all lies.

They used to say that witches could cast spells
And cause great harm,
They used to say wise women could enchant you
With a charm.

So, the men would come with pitch forks and take the witches off to jail,
They accused them of doing magic tricks and causing farmers crops to fail.

But these were just wise women, like my nanny,
They were gentle, kind, and good,
They could not cast a wicked spell like the stories said they could.

Nanny does not have an evil laugh.
Or warts upon her chin
She does not keep the eyes of toads inside a metal tin.

My nanny loves me very much,
And is always by my side,
With her words of gentle wisdom,
That will often be my guide.

So, don't believe the stories that you hear,
For most are just not true,
And I bet, that if you are lucky,
Your nanny is a wise Witch too.

About the Author

Lynsey, an Emotional Wellbeing and Mindfulness Coach from Cheshire, is part of a women's group called *The Silver Spoons Collective*.

Together, during the 2020 lockdown, they created an exhibition of art, film and dance called *I Am Witch*.

This exhibition will tour the UK from 2022 with an aim to educate, empower women, and heal the trauma passed down to us from the Burning Times of the 16th and 17th centuries.

This is Lynsey's first book, and was created as a gift for her grandson James, and also as her own exhibit piece.

To find out more, visit **www.facebook.com/silverspoonscollective** or connect with Lynsey on Instagram: **www.instagram.com/lynseytidbury.**

Printed in Great Britain
by Amazon